Adventures of
Fred in the Shed

by Lynette Wynn

AuthorHouse™
1663 Liberty Drive
Bloomington, IN 47403
www.authorhouse.com
Phone: 1 (800) 839-8640

Published by AuthorHouse 10/10/2016

ISBN: 978-1-5246-4285-3 (sc)
ISBN: 978-1-5246-4286-0 (e)

Library of Congress Control Number: 2016916412

Print information available on the last page.

Any people depicted in stock imagery provided by Thinkstock are models,
and such images are being used for illustrative purposes only.
Certain stock imagery © Thinkstock.

This book is printed on acid-free paper.

authorHOUSE®

Hello! My name is Fred, and I live in Lucy's shed.

I was discovered one day when Lucy went into the shed with her mother to get some gardening tools. Lucy's mother said "I think we have a little guest living in here. "Look over there," as she pointed to the little droppings I must have left behind the night before during my search for food. I really did not mean to leave a mess, but when ya gotta go, ya gotta go!

Later that night, after dark, I heard a noise. The door opened, and I heard rustling and whispered voices. Someone put something on the floor of the shed. I could smell that something was different. When the rustling and voices stopped and the door closed I crawled out from my corner of the shed to inspect what had been left there. I expected to find one of those nasty sticky traps that many of my friends have been caught in.

Much to my surprise, I found a small dish with fresh water and an even bigger dish full of treats waiting for me. I moved closer very slowly to inspect the offering. I wanted to make sure it was safe and not a trap. I was so excited that I danced around the shed for ten minutes.

I could not believe my luck. There were apples, grapes, cookies, pretzels, peanuts, cereal, pasta, bread, muffins, meat, and so much more! It was like a Thanksgiving and Christmas feast all in one night. I ran back home and told my family what I had found. This was a feast for my family. I told everyone, "Get your backpacks and fill both cheeks so we can take it all back to our nest."

We all made many trips, collecting our newfound feast, and were very tired after moving all the food back to our nest. Before going to bed, we unloaded everything and ate until our bellies were full. It was the most wonderful, delicious dinner we'd had in a very long time. Up until Lucy surprised us with so much food, I was having a hard time trying to feed all of my family. We are a large family with many babies. Sometimes my children will move out, but others always seem to stick around.

It has been over a year now that our friend Lucy has been giving us treats. It does not matter what the weather is outside; Lucy always delivers our dinner. When the water dish is empty, I drag it out to the middle of the floor, and Lucy refills it for the next night. She seems to understand just what I want.

Lucy has been coming into the shed after dark with our dinner. She says, "C'mon, Fred, get your dinner." We all rush out to see what is on the buffet for that night.

Sometimes I get impatient and sit on the windowsill, licking my lips in anticipation and waiting for Lucy to come down the sidewalk with a flashlight to give us our dinner. When she opens the door, I run into the corner so she doesn't notice me. I don't want to look desperate or greedy. When the moon is out, it is very bright in the shed, and I can see everything in the dish. My children are especially fond of the cookies and always go for them first. My family and I are so grateful to Lucy that she decided to take care of us instead of get rid of us.

We try to not leave any more droppings as we go for our nightly buffet. I told my family to be respectful and not destroy anything in the shed.

During the daytime hours we can sneak out of the shed through a crack under the door. We make sure the coast is clear from any bad animals who might want to hurt us.

There is a pile of bird seed not far from the door, and we enjoy that as an afternoon snack before our naps. I have told my family that if we do not clean our part of the shed, Lucy might get mad and not bring us treats anymore.

One day while we were taking care of our housekeeping duties, another animal came into the shed. It snuck under the same crack that we use to go out to eat the birdseed. It was a little larger than us. We all stopped and stared. We were afraid at first, but then he smiled and introduced himself. "My name is Snickels," he said. "I'm a chipmunk."

My children ran up to Snickels, wanting to make friends right away. They were so excited about having someone new to play with instead of just their brothers and sisters.

"I eat the birdseed when Lucy is not around," Snickels said.

"We also eat the birdseed," I told him, "as a snack."

Snickels pointed to the birdseed bucket that Lucy stored in the shed. "I'd like to get in there," he said, "but I'm not strong enough to lift the lid by myself. Will you please help me?"

We all got together and tried to lift the lid, but it was still too heavy.

Sometimes Snickels and my children run and play in the yard. My children love the stripes on Snickels's sides. "You look like a racer!" one of my children said.

"Maybe that is why I'm so fast," Snickels answered.

When we told Snickels about the buffet from Lucy, he nodded and said, "She has been feeding me treats for years. Lucy gives me peanuts and sunflower seeds as special treats. She makes a squeaky noise when she has peanuts for me, and I go running into the yard or up onto her porch. Sometimes there are peanuts stuck between Lucy's bare toes that I have to pull out." He giggled and said, "At least her feet don't stink, and her toes are soft. I even let her pet me sometimes, as long as she is very gentle. You have to trust the human occasionally to get the good treats. Lucy will throw peanuts to me in the yard for hours on end, sometimes even until it is dark."

Lucy seems to love all the critters in her yard and would never hurt any of them. Snickels asked us if we get fed every night. I told him, "Lucy has not missed a single night since she started to feed us. She even comes out to feed us when it is raining or snowing.

"When it gets really cold outside each year," Snickels told us, "I sleep underground for about four to five months."

Our eyes grew wide with surprise. "How can you do that?" I asked.

"My heartbeat drops so low that I don't even get hungry," he answered.

I shook my head. "I still don't know how you can *not* eat every day. You don't know what you are missing!"

Snickels shrugged. "That is what chipmunks do, just like mice eat mostly during the night. My entire house is underground. I have a pantry, kitchen, bathroom, living room, and a bedroom. I clean my house every morning and then take out my trash. My bed is lined with soft fur and hair that I found from different animals around the yard. I have many tunnels that stretch all over the yard that I use for my living quarters. I also have many entrances and escape routes in case anything chases me or tries to catch me, like cats or big birds from the sky."

"I've also been chased by those bad animals," I said to Snickels, "and have to run very fast to escape."

I invited Snickels to see our house, which has a big bedroom in the corner of the shed for all the family. "Our bed is also lined with fur and hair that we found outside," I said. "The rest of the house is in Lucy's shed."

"Can you see at night?" Snickels suddenly asked me.

"Why, of course I can," I replied. "How do you think we find the dish to eat our buffet?"

"I can't see very well at night," Snickels said. "Right before it gets totally dark, I get ready for bed. Sometimes at night, before the sun completely goes down, I politely ask a lightning bug to sit on my back to go into the tunnels, just to make sure everything is all right before I settle down for the night."

As we were sitting around talking and getting to know each other better, Snickels told us about one of his adventures in Lucy's yard. One morning just as the sun was coming up, Snickels came out of his hole to stretch and take a bath, using the dew from the grass. As he looked around, he came face-to-face with a new creature. He stopped dead in his tracks. This creature was much, much larger than Snickels, and very scary-looking. They stared at each other for a few minutes. The new creature broke eye contact first and continued eating its breakfast of dewy grass. Snickels said, "Who are you, and what are you doing in my yard?"

The creature said, "I am a girl bunny, and my name is Blaze. Who and what are you, and why are you so small?"

"I'm Snickels, and I'm a chipmunk. I live in the yard, underground, with many tunnels."

"I live in the corner of the yard with my brothers and sisters," said Blaze. "It's a small hole that my mommy dug, and it is lined with soft fur from Mommy's belly."

"I have some soft fur in my bed too," Snickels said. Then he looked closer at Blaze and asked, "What is that white mark on your forehead. Does it hurt?

"It's a birthmark of white fur," Blaze answered. "I don't like, it but that's how I got my name."

"It looks very pretty on you. A birthmark is nothing to be ashamed of." Snickels then asked Blaze if she wanted to be friends, and Blaze readily accepted the offer.

"I have a few brothers and sisters back at our nest," she said. "Can they be your friend too?"

"That's fine with me," Snickels said. "The more friends the better. You can never have too many friends. I have another new friend. His name is Fred. I met him and his family in the shed a few weeks ago. If you think I am small, you will really be surprised at their size. Fred could easily fit in your mouth, and no one would ever see him."

Blaze wrinkled her nose. "No thanks. I don't eat meat, but I would very much like to meet them. I come out mainly in the early morning or just before the sun goes down. It is too hot for me in the afternoon, and there is a scary thing in the sky that tries to catch me. There also is a big thing that walks around the yard, talking to me sometimes. I'm not sure what to make of it or if I can trust it."

Snickels just laughed and said, "That is just Lucy; she is our *big* friend who walks on only two feet. Imagine how hard and uncomfortable that would be to do if you could not hop. Lucy feeds all of the critters in the yard."

"Maybe that's where the carrots and lettuce come from sometimes," Blaze said.

Snickels agreed. "Probably so."

Blaze said, "I eat birdseed and get water from a dish down by the big building at night when I get tired of eating grass and there isn't anything else around."

"That's all from Lucy too," Snickels told Blaze. "Fred and his family also eat the birdseed, along with all the birds—it's really intended for them."

It was an exciting and interesting morning for both of them, but they had chores and other things to do, so after visiting for a while, they decided to go their separate ways for the day. They made plans to have a picnic later in the week and to include Fred and his family and anyone else in the yard that wanted to join. They wondered if maybe they would meet someone else new and be off on another adventure.

We all have a very good life here in the shed and yard. We are comfortable, well fed, and have much love from Lucy, our families, and new friends. What more could we ask for?

We are all very lucky to have a protector-friend like Lucy. We will never take her kindness and the treats she provides for granted.

About the Author

Lynette Wynn lives in a small town in Pennsylvania. Like many animal lovers, she feeds and cares for all the animals with feathers or fur that come into her yard. She provides food, water, and shelter, as well as the occasional doctoring of anything that might need her help.

This story is about a few of those animals that she has become especially attached to over the years, which she considers almost like her children.

Lynette's husband and mother encouraged her to write a book about the animal adventures that have occurred over the years. She thanks them for their continued encouragement and support in the writing of this book.

Alyson, Nathan & Lucy

Enjoy Fred & his friends!

Lynette Lynn
Linda Bergau

Edwards Brothers Malloy
Thorofare, NJ USA
October 25, 2016